Two-Minute GARFIELD Stories

Created by Jim Davis
Stories by Jim Kraft
Illustrated by Mike Fentz

A GOLDEN BOOK • NEW YORK

Western Publishing Company, Inc., Racine, Wisconsin 53404

Garfield and the Spider

Garfield yawned. "Boy, am I tired," he said. "I haven't slept in minutes." He pulled back the blanket on his bed—and screamed!

There was a big, hairy spider on his pillow!

"I hate spiders!" cried Garfield. He waved his paw at the spider. "Scram!" he said. "Go sit on a tuffet or something." But the spider just sat there grinning.

Garfield needed something to get rid of the spider. Unfortunately, Jon was all out of spider spray. So Garfield tried hair spray. It didn't drive the spider away, but it *did* make his hair look nice.

Next Garfield tried luring the spider out of bed with a chocolate chip cookie. But the spider made a face and didn't budge.

"This spider is really starting to bug me," said Garfield. "It's time to get serious."

Garfield placed a stepladder next to his bed. Then he rolled Jon's bowling ball out of the closet. Grunting and groaning, Garfield dragged the bowling ball up to the top of the ladder.

"You've had your chance, Fang Face," Garfield said to the spider. "Now it's Splat City for you!" He shoved the bowling ball off the ladder.

The heavy ball crashed down, smashing Garfield's bed—but not the spider. He just scurried away at the last moment.

"Well, at least I got my bed back," said Garfield. "Too bad I didn't get it back in one piece. But that spider won't mess with *me* again. Time for a nice, peaceful nap!"

Worst Impressions

Garfield was lounging in his front yard one morning when he saw Arlene coming down the street.

"Arlene has barely noticed how wonderful I am lately," thought Garfield. "I should do something to impress her."

So, as she walked by, Garfield yelled, "Hey, Arlene!" while making his goofiest face.

Arlene only frowned at Garfield and walked on.

Garfield followed her to
the park, where his impression
of a fountain made
no impression on Arlene.

His Frisbee-catching
didn't catch her eye, either.

"This will do it," said Garfield.
He started to swing on the swings.
He swung very high. Then he jumped
right off the swing!

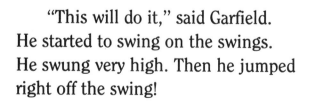

Whomp! Garfield landed hard on his furry face.

"Garfield, are you all right?" asked Arlene.

"I suppose," said Garfield. "Fortunately, fat doesn't break. Did I impress you?"

"I'm not impressed with goofy faces and stupid stunts," said Arlene. "I like it when someone is nice and talks to me in a normal way."

Garfield thought for a moment. Then he said, "How are you today, Arlene?"

"Now I'm impressed," said Arlene.

World's Best Garfield

 Garfield snapped off the awards program he and Odie had been watching on television. "Seems like people are always getting awards for being the best at something," he said to Odie. "I'd like to get an award, too. I'd like to get *lots* of awards. So, do you know what I'm going to do? Tomorrow I'm going to start being the best at *everything*."

Garfield actually got up early
the next day. First he decided
to be the best athlete in the world.
But he wasn't so good at soccer.

At basketball he was
even worse.

The hurdles were, well,
too much of a hurdle.

Next Garfield tried being the world's best thinker. But all he could think about was lunch.

He would have been the world's best video-game player, but the Zarkoids vaporized his star cruiser.

As for Garfield's singing, the neighbors thought it was definitely the world's worst!

"I give up," Garfield moaned to Odie. "I'll never be the best at anything. I'll just be a fat, lazy, lovable cat."

Odie gave Garfield a big lick.

"Thanks, Odie," said Garfield. "Now I think I'll eat everything in the refrigerator and sleep until next Tuesday."

Suddenly, Garfield's face brightened. "Wait a minute! I may be just a fat, lazy, lovable cat, but I'm the *best* fat, lazy, lovable cat I know."

Odie barked in agreement.

Garfield was happy again. He didn't have to be the world's best athlete or singer. He was already the world's best—and only—Garfield!

No Dogs Allowed

One day, while he was prowling through a vacant lot, Garfield came upon a large, empty cardboard box. "This is just what I've been looking for," he thought. "It will make a perfect clubhouse."

Garfield cut windows and a door into the box. He found an old crate to use as a table and a bucket for a stool. Then he painted a sign over the door. It said, "GARFIELD'S CLUB—NO DOGS ALLOWED!"

Garfield was about to hold his first club meeting when Odie stuck his nose in the door. "Hey, don't you see the sign?" cried Garfield. "No mutts in my clubhouse!" Odie's ears drooped sadly as he shuffled away.

A short time later, as he was voting on whether to eat cookies or pizza at the next meeting, Garfield was interrupted by hammering noises.

Odie had found an old packing crate and was building a clubhouse of his own—right next to Garfield's!

"That's a pretty neat clubhouse," Garfield said. "Mind if I look inside?"

But Odie growled and pointed to a sign he had made. It said, "Odie's Club—No Garfields Allowed!"

"Who cares?" said Garfield, stomping off. "My club is better anyway."

Garfield and Odie sat in their clubhouses, each one staring out his own little window. They sat like that for a long time. Finally Garfield sighed. So did Odie.

"This club would be more fun if it had another member," said Garfield, loud enough so Odie could hear.

"Arf!" agreed Odie.

In no time at all, they converted the two small clubhouses into one big clubhouse. Then they took down the old signs and put up a new one. It said, "GARFIELD AND ODIE'S CLUB—FRIENDS WELCOME!"

Snack Attack!

Bong! Bong! The clock struck midnight. Garfield slowly opened his eyes and smiled. "Time to rise and dine," he said with a yawn.

Garfield padded to the kitchen. He opened the refrigerator, which was filled with food. "I can't decide what to eat," he thought. "I guess I'll just have to eat everything!"

"Keep your paws off her!" ordered a voice.

"Who said that?" asked Garfield.

"I did," replied a slice of lasagna.

"Yeah, leave that pie alone," added a hot dog.

"We're tired of you gobbling us up every night," said the lasagna. "And we're not going to take it anymore. Come on, gang, let's get the cat!"

A mob of food leapt out of the refrigerator and began to chase Garfield around the house.

"I hate it when food goes bad," puffed Garfield.

The food captured Garfield. They tied him up on a big platter.

"OK, who wants a leg?" asked the hot dog.

"A leg?" said Garfield. "You mean, you're going to eat me?"

"It's only fair," replied the lasagna. "You've been munching on us for years."

"Wait!" cried Garfield. "Fatty foods aren't good for you! HELP!"

Suddenly, Garfield woke up. He was in his bed. There was no food in sight.

"Dreaming about food makes me hungry," he said. "I need a snack." Garfield started to get out of bed. "On second thought, I'll wait until breakfast," he said. "Midnight snacks can come back to haunt you!"

Rainy-Day Fun

Garfield and Odie stared out the window and sighed.

"Why did it have to rain today?" asked Garfield glumly. "I really wanted to go out. Now we'll be stuck inside with Jon. That should be a real yawn."

"Garfield! Odie!" called Jon. "Want to watch me iron my underwear?"

Garfield cringed. "I can't stand it," he said.

Nothing in the house interested Garfield.
He flipped through 148 TV channels.
"I've seen all these shows," he grumbled.
"I've read all of the books here and
I've played all the games. I've tied all
the fun stuff to Odie's tongue. Aaargh!
I'm bored with being inside!"

Suddenly Garfield had an idea. "Come on, Odie," he said. "Let's get
wet!"

Garfield and Odie put on their raincoats, rainhats, and galoshes and ran out the door. Garfield jumped into a big puddle. Odie jumped in behind him. They stomped in the puddle and laughed as the water sloshed all around.

"Who says you need sunshine to have a good time?" asked Garfield.

Garfield found an old box, and the two pets climbed inside. They pretended that they were brave fishermen on the stormy ocean. They pretended so well that Odie felt seasick!

"It's still a great day for baseball!" cried Garfield. But it wasn't easy throwing the ball over home plate when home plate kept floating away!

After a few hours of rainy play, the two pets were very wet and very tired.

"There you are!" cried Jon when Garfield and Odie stepped inside. "Just look at you! Why did you go out in this awful weather?"

Garfield and Odie smiled at each other. "Well, Jon," replied Garfield, "I guess we just wanted to soak up some fun!"

Odie Finds a Friend

Odie was sniffing around the yard one afternoon when suddenly he found himself nose-to-beak with a little bird.

The pup and the bird eyed each other curiously.

"Tweet?" said the bird.

"Arf?" barked Odie.

Odie followed the little bird around the yard. When the little bird plucked a worm from the ground, Odie plucked a worm, too—though he couldn't bring himself to eat it.

When the little bird splashed in the birdbath, so did Odie—though he nearly splashed the little bird right out of the bath.

And when the little bird sang on the fence, Odie sang along, too—though his "singing" wasn't all that musical.

But when the little bird
flew high up into the sky,
Odie was left behind. His ears
drooped. Whimpering softly, he trudged
across the yard and sprawled in the shade of the big oak tree.

Odie sighed. He'd been
having such fun with the little
bird. But she was probably
gone forever.

The next day, Odie heard a familiar
chirp. It was the little bird!
She glided down to a gentle
landing on Odie's nose.

"Tweet!" said the little bird.

"Arf!" barked Odie. And
he wagged his tail happily,
for now he knew that he had found a friend.

Good Night, Garfield!

The grandfather clock struck nine o'clock. Garfield yawned. "Time to say good night," he said.

"Good night, chair. Good night, TV. Thanks for staying up with me.

"Good night, refrigerator. Good night, bowl. In the morning could you please be full?

"Good night, Odie. Sleep tight, old friend. Tomorrow I'll pull your tail again.

"Good night, Pooky, my teddy bear. It's good to know you're always there.

"Good night, blanket. Good night, bed. It's time to rest my sleepy head.

"It's time to dream. But before I do, it's time to say good night to *you*! "GOOD NIGHT!"